Jim's Dog, Muffins

By Miriam Cohen
Illustrated by Ronald Himler

Star Bright Books
New York

Published in the United States of America by Star Bright Books, Inc., New York. The name Star Bright Books and the Star Bright Books logo are registered trademarks of Star Bright Books, Inc. Please visit www.starbrightbooks.com.

Hardback ISBN-13: 978-1-59572-099-3
Paperback ISBN-13: 978-1-59572-100-6

Previously published under ISBN 0440411246

Printed in China (WKT) 9 8 7 6 5 4 3 2 1

Library of Congress Cataloging-in-Publication Data is available.

For Dr. Edith Weigart—
"Nature will say, 'Don't cry anymore.'"—M.C.

"Jim's dog got killed by the garbage truck!
It was all squashed!
Jim's not coming to school today."
Danny was telling everybody about it.

"Did Jim cry?" Paul asked.

"No," Danny said.

"But he wouldn't talk to anybody."

The teacher said, "Jim must be very sad.
If we write a letter to him,
it might help him feel better."

The teacher wrote
what they said.

Dear Jim,

We wish Muffins didn't die.
She was a nice dog.

Love,

Danny, Paul, Louie, Sammy,
Sara, Margaret

After school, the teacher
took the letter to Jim's house.

When Jim came back, he wouldn't talk to anybody. That morning they gave their whale reports.

Louie said, "Whales never bite you."

And Paul said whales can even sing.
But Jim wasn't listening.
He was thinking about Muffins.

The home-making teacher came in with bags of carrots, onions, parsley, and potatoes.

"We're going to cook vegetable soup today."

Everybody was waiting for the soup
to be cooked, except Jim.
He was looking out the window.

When the soup was ready, they invited the principal to have lunch with them. They sat down at the table and the principal and the teacher started to eat. "Oh, this is so good," they said.

But Danny said, "there is something in here! What is it? Yech! Parsley!"
And he began to take every piece of parsley out of his soup. By the time he got it all out, lunch was over.

At recess, Jim sat on a bench.
Louie and Sammy came over to see him.
"Maybe you'll forget Muffins, Jim?"
Jim shook his head.

Danny put his arm around Jim.
"Don't worry," he said.
"I'm never going to die."
Jim didn't say anything.

Anna Maria sat down on the bench next to him.
"It doesn't do any good to be sad," she said.

Jim yelled, "Shut up! Get away!"
And he pushed Anna Maria off
the bench.

Anna Maria started screaming.
When the teacher came, she cried,
"I was just trying to make him
feel better!"

The teacher said,
"Maybe Jim needs time to feel sad."

Jim stayed by himself.
If anybody came near, he covered his ears.
And Anna Maria told them, "Don't play with him."

Jim didn't even choose a book
when it was time for the whole
school to stop and read. He just sat.

After school, Jim started home again.

Paul ran after him. "My father gave me
money for two slices of pizza. Come on, Jim."
"I don't want any," Jim said.

The pizza smell came around the corner.
When they came to the store, Paul stopped.
"Two slices please," he said.

He gave one to Jim. Jim just held it.
Then Paul did what he always did.
He pushed a lot of pizza into his mouth.

Jim looked at Paul. He took
one bite. Then he began pushing
pizza in. They began to laugh.
They laughed and laughed.

Jim said, "Remember how I used
to give Muffins the crust?"
Tears came down on his pizza,
but he kept on eating.

"She was the nicest dog," Paul said.
"Yes," said Jim.
And they walked home together.